Holiday!

by
Rowan McAuley

Illustrations by
Aki Fukuoka

hardie grant EGMONT

Chapter One

Iris was in her room playing her saxophone. She was learning a new piece for the school band, and the fingering was really tricky.

She was concentrating so hard that she didn't notice her mum had come in until she was standing right in front of the music stand.

Iris jumped and blew a weird-sounding raspberry through the sax.

'Mum!' she squealed. 'Don't sneak up on me!'

Her mum sighed. 'Not you, too! Kick's just told me off for the same thing.'

Iris looked past her mum to the doorway. There was her little brother, Kick, grinning and giving her the thumbs up with one hand, while he hooked his hearing aids back over his ears with the other.

'Cool, huh?' he said.

Iris turned back to her mum. 'What's cool? What's going on? You *never* interrupt me while I'm practising.'

'Well …' said her mum, but before she could say another word, Kick blurted it out.

'We're going on holiday!'

'Really?' Iris asked, putting down her sax. Kick was always telling dumb jokes, and she thought this might be one of them. 'When? Where? And why?'

Her mum smiled. 'It's very last minute, but Dad just called to say that his boss needs him to do a big presentation tomorrow at the head office, not all that far from where Nan and Pa live,' she said.

'So we thought, why don't we all go and make the trip a family holiday?'

Iris laughed in delight. 'No way! Nan and Pa? Excellent!'

She hardly ever saw her grandparents, so when she did they always spoilt her and Kick rotten.

'The only problem,' their mum went on, 'is that school doesn't break up until the end of the week, so –'

Iris froze. *Please don't say it's not going to work*, she begged silently. *Don't tease us with a holiday and then say we can't go!*

'I've already spoken with Ms Kyle,' her mum said calmly. 'And she's not worried if you both miss a couple of days this week.'

'YAAAY!' shrieked Iris, dancing around in a circle. Kick, who was always ready to go crazy, came over and danced with her, whooping and clapping.

After a while, Iris and Kick settled down. There was only so much celebrating

Iris could do before she realised she had a ton of questions to ask.

'So, Kick,' Iris said as she pushed her hair off her face. 'When do we leave?'

Kick shrugged.

'Well, then, how long are we going for?' she tried.

Kick shrugged again. 'Mum didn't tell me,' he said. 'She wanted to tell us together.'

'Oh.' Iris looked around. 'Where has Mum gone, then?'

Iris went off to find her, with Kick following behind. Their mum was in her bedroom, with two suitcases on the bed and the wardrobe doors open.

'Hey, Mum,' said Iris. 'Kick and I were

wondering what the plan is.'

'Were you now?' her mum smiled. 'I was wondering when you'd want to know.'

Iris and Kick stood by the bed, watching as their mum folded T-shirts, trousers and a skirt and laid them carefully in the suitcases.

'Well,' she said as she packed. 'Dad's meeting is early in the morning, so we haven't got much time to get going.'

Almost none at all, thought Iris. On their last visit to see Nan and Pa, it had taken a whole day and a whole night to drive there. *So, for this holiday, we'll have to leave before dinner tonight to make it in time.*

'Dad has to work back late tonight

to get everything ready for his meeting, so we won't be driving,' Iris's mum explained. 'We're going by plane instead. And we'll all stay at Dad's hotel for the first night.'

This was unbelievable! Iris had never been on a plane before.

She didn't just shriek, she *screamed.*

'A *plane!* A *hotel!* Awesome!'

Chapter Two

While Iris's dad was working at his office late that night, Iris, her mum and Kick started packing. They also began tidying up because their mum said she liked to return to a spotless house after being on holiday.

And, of course, Iris had to call all her friends to let them know she wouldn't be at school for the next two days.

She was calling her best friend, Zoe, as her mum was glaring into the fridge.

'I can't believe I did a full shop this morning. Look! The fridge is absolutely packed, and we won't be here to eat it.'

'Yeah, annoying,' Iris said, only half-listening to her mum as she waited for someone at Zoe's to pick up the phone. Iris knew her mum hated wasting food, but a holiday was surely worth a mouldy loaf of bread, wasn't it?

Zoe finally answered. 'Hello,' she puffed, as if she'd been running for miles. 'Zoe speaking.'

'Hello, Zoe speaking!' teased Iris. 'I was about to hang up. Guess what?'

Iris quickly told Zoe the news, and Zoe said excitedly that Iris would totally love the hotel bathroom. Zoe had stayed in hotels before and always brought back the tiny soaps and mini shampoo bottles that hotels put out for guests to use.

Iris glanced at the clock on the microwave. 'Better go, Zo,' she said. 'I've still got to pack and I haven't called Isabelle yet.'

The more Iris thought about it, the more there was for her to do. She'd have to clean out the fish tank in her room or it would be really gross by the time she got back.

She also wanted to tidy up her room a bit, so it would be nice to come home to. And she had to phone Mia and Siri to say she wouldn't be around after all for the sleep-over they had planned for the school holidays …

Boy, going on a holiday is a lot of work, she thought, pulling her favourite bag out from under her bed so she could start packing.

But the hard work didn't seem like a big deal at all when she thought about flying on a plane and staying in a hotel, and then about the great time ahead with her nan and pa. She felt so happy and excited about the holiday, she couldn't imagine grumbling about a bit of tidying up ever again.

A plane! Iris kept whispering to herself in amazement. *How cool!*

The next morning Iris woke up so early that it was still grey outside. She felt incredibly happy and bubbly, but for a second she couldn't remember why. Then it hit her.

It's today! Iris smiled to herself. *We're going on holiday, and I didn't dream it because there's my bag — all packed and ready.*

She bounced out of bed and pulled on the outfit she had laid out ready the night before. Then she practically skipped down the hallway.

She could already tell it was going to be the most perfect day. She would be doing about a hundred things she'd never done before, starting with getting a taxi to the airport. And she still had ten dollars in her back pocket, left over from her birthday and ready to use for holiday shopping. *Excellent!*

'Iris!' her mum called. 'Can you please

wake Kick up? He needs breakfast before we go.'

Iris caught a whiff of the bacon and mushrooms her dad was frying up in the kitchen, and her mouth watered as she ran to get her brother. Things kept getting better and better!

Chapter Three

After a massive breakfast, where their parents tried to get Iris and Kick to eat practically everything in the fridge, Iris took a box of vegies and the leftover bread and milk next door to Mr Calder. She got back just in time to check that her bag was zipped up properly before the taxi came.

It felt like a dream to be winding her way through the city to the airport at exactly the time Iris and Kick would normally be catching the bus to school. And it was so cool to be having her bags weighed at the airport check-in desk at exactly the same time that she would normally be lining up in the playground for roll call.

At the check-in desk, Iris watched her luggage roll along a conveyer belt and then disappear through a wobbly black rubber curtain.

Then her dad led them through the security check. That meant any luggage they wanted to carry onto the plane with them had to be put through a big X-ray machine, while they had to walk under a special scanner that beeped if they had anything metal in their pockets.

This is so cool, Iris thought, smiling to herself as she tightly grasped onto her boarding pass ('Do *not* lose it!' her mum had warned her).

After the security check, the family headed down the longest corridor Iris had ever seen. It stretched on so far, she couldn't quite see the end of it. Along the sides were coffee shops and sushi bars, and in between were big lounge areas full of seats and waiting passengers.

'Our plane's right down the end,' Iris's dad said after he had checked his boarding pass. Iris noticed there were funny flat escalators along the length of the corridor, a bit like conveyer belts for people. She saw adults in business suits walking along them, looking very serious and important.

'Can we do that?' she asked her dad.

'You mean hop on the travelators?' he replied. 'Go ahead.'

'Come on, Kick,' grinned Iris. 'Let's do it!'

She sped ahead of her mum and dad, and power-walked along the travelators with Kick beside her. It was almost like being a superhero, striding along at top speed. She imagined she was rushing off to catch a plane on her own – a star sax player, flying off to a concert on the other side of the world, with hundreds of fans and a limousine waiting for her.

She'd never felt so glamorous in her life!

They got to the end of the corridor, and Iris stepped off the last travelator. She was disappointed for a second at how heavy and ordinary it felt to walk along the carpet. But the disappointment was immediately replaced with excitement when her dad bought her and Kick hot chocolates at the cafe next to their lounge, and Iris saw two pilots walk by in their uniforms.

Then she and Kick stood by the gigantic windows and watched planes taking off and landing, and being loaded and unloaded with bags, until it was time for them to board.

Iris handed the flight attendant her boarding pass, and then followed her mum down a carpeted tunnel. It went around corners and sloped downwards until it reached the plane. Kick and her dad followed behind.

Oh, this is a bit scary.

Iris had a little tremor of nerves as she stepped into the plane. A cold breeze was whistling through a gap between the open door of the plane and the tunnel, and she shivered.

I'm really doing this, she thought suddenly. *I'm really on an aeroplane now!*

Chapter Four

Iris followed her mum down the narrow aisle of the plane until they got to their seats in row twenty-one. The plane was so crowded! Worse than the school bus, with everyone trying to squeeze past to get to their seats, bumping into each other and saying, 'Sorry! Sorry!' about a million times.

'Who's got the window seat?' their mum asked.

'Me!' said Iris and Kick at exactly the same time.

'No way! Not you – me!' Their voices came together in a muddle.

Iris was in front of Kick, so she got to slide right into the window seat.

Kick flopped crossly into the seat next to her. 'That's so unfair!' he grouched.

'Relax, Kick,' said their mum. 'How about if Iris sits there for take-off, and you swap halfway through the flight? That way you can have the window for landing.'

'Good,' said Kick sourly, obviously still grumpy.

'Iris?' her dad asked.

'Yeah, OK,' Iris said easily. She wasn't

about to let a little thing like that get her holiday off to a bad start.

Still, she thought, *Kick shouldn't make such a fuss when he misses out on something he wants. It wouldn't kill him to grow up a bit.*

Take-off was awesome. The plane moved slowly past the airport until it reached the runway, and then there was a pause while the cabin crew showed the passengers how to put on their life jackets.

Iris's eyes bulged in alarm and she looked over at her mum.

'It's just in case, Iris,' her mum said quietly. 'But we're not going to need them.'

After the crew had sat down, the plane began to move faster. Much faster. The engines screamed louder and louder, and the wheels rumbled like thunder on the runway.

Iris stared out the window at the ground flashing by. The plane bumped and swayed a bit, and then ... nothing.

The rumbling and bumping had stopped, and Iris realised that they were above the ground. Actually flying!

Iris watched as the houses and roads shrank down to the size of a model village, and then became even smaller, as if they were part of a satellite photo of the earth. The plane flew so high that she could see whole rivers at once and the hills and valleys looked like wrinkles in a blanket.

Then they went right through the

clouds! It was misty and grey for a few moments, and then – *wow!* Iris hadn't expected anything so beautiful. There was wide blue sky above them, and the clouds beneath were so fat and white and fluffy that Iris wanted to run and bounce on them as though they were a giant jumping castle.

She gazed out the window dreamily. It didn't seem nearly long enough before Kick jabbed her with his elbow and said, 'Time's up! My turn for the window.'

After playing three games of spit with her mum, and eating a tray of the tiniest, cutest sandwiches ever, Iris's ears began to feel stuffy and blocked.

Her stomach swooped a little, like she was on a swing, and her dad said, 'We've started to descend. We'll be landing soon.' His voice sounded like it was coming from miles away.

'What?' Iris said.

Her dad smiled. 'Yawn as big as you can. It will help pop your ears. Or hold your nose while you blow. That works, too.'

Iris tried it. It was seriously weird! She blew her nose and held it at the same time, like her head was a balloon that she was blowing up from the inside, and then, *pop!* She could hear again.

Her stomach swooped again as the plane dropped lower, and she bit her lip. She couldn't tell if she was excited or scared, so she decided that landing was full of scary excitement!

Iris thought taking off would make her nervous, but it was landing that got to her. But she soon learnt to ignore the screaming sound of the engines.

And it's OK once you accept the fact that

your big-headed brother won't lean back so you can see out the window as well, she thought.

Chapter Five

After they'd all gotten their bags off the luggage carousel, Iris's dad took a taxi to his meeting while everyone else headed to the hotel.

And what a hotel! Iris gaped. There was a man in a lovely deep green uniform standing by the front doors, waiting to carry their bags. Inside, the lobby was like something from one of those travel shows on TV. There were giant vases of flowers everywhere, coffee tables and leather furniture by the windows, and sparkling gift stores by the lifts. It was all so hushed and calm and *elegant*.

Iris stood up very straight, and tried to tiptoe across the shiny floor as they walked to the reception desk. Beside her, Kick dragged his feet and said loudly, 'Mum, I really, *really* need the toilet.'

Iris couldn't believe it. 'Kick!' she hissed. 'Shh!'

'What?' said Kick, even louder. 'I'm just saying, I'm really, really desperate for a —'

'Be quiet!' Iris glared at him. She was

whispering so low Kick would have to lip-read. 'You don't have to be so noisy all the time.'

Kick just rolled his eyes at her.

'All right, guys,' said their mum, turning away from the reception desk. 'We've got our room key. Let's go!'

Iris gave Kick one last scowl, and then smiled brilliantly at her mum. 'Cool. I can't wait.'

'Neither can I,' said Kick. 'And I mean, I *really* can't wait.'

Iris tried to ignore him. *What a pain!*

The hotel room was brilliant! Iris had thought a hotel room would be exactly what it sounded like – one room. But they had something that looked more like a whole apartment. They had a little kitchen with a dishwasher and a microwave, and a sitting room with a TV, two sofas *and* a balcony. And there was one bedroom for her mum and dad, and one for her and Kick.

Wait till I tell Zoe about the hotel!

Iris remembered what Zoe had said about hotels, and went to check out their bathroom while Kick was on the balcony. She wanted to poke around a bit without him following her.

The bathroom was at the end of the corridor, and when Iris opened the door all she could say was, 'Wow.'

'Hey! What?' Kick had suddenly appeared out of nowhere.

Iris ground her teeth in frustration. For a deaf kid, he was pretty hard to sneak off from.

Still, it was actually good to be able to share her excitement with him. 'Look,' she said, pointing. There on the shelf by the mirror were almost a dozen tiny bottles. They went closer to read the labels.

'Shampoo, conditioner, moisturiser,' Iris said out loud. 'Oh, look – you can choose between pine needles and sea salt for boys, or apricot blossom and vanilla for girls.'

'And matching soap!' said Kick. 'Little bars, all in wrappers.'

'Ooh, and look at the towels!' Iris added.

The railing by the bath was heaped with huge, fluffy white towels. There was a stack of smaller ones for drying your hands or wrapping your wet hair in.

'You know, with this many towels you

wouldn't need to wrap yourself in one towel like a normal person,' said Iris. 'You could just make a huge pile on the floor and then *roll* in them.'

'Well, don't get used to it,' their mum laughed as she stood in the doorway. 'This is only for one night. Tomorrow we check out and go to stay with Nan and Pa.'

'Nan and Pa!' yelped Iris. 'They said to call and let them know when we'd arrived at the hotel! Can I phone them?'

'Definitely,' said her mum. 'And when you've done that, you can come downstairs with me and find a newspaper. Dad won't be back till late this afternoon, so the three of us are going to find a movie to see.'

Iris felt as though she could float away
like a balloon with all the happiness inside
her. Could this holiday get any better?

Chapter Six

Downstairs in the lobby, Iris, her mum and Kick looked around for a newspaper.

'There,' whispered Iris, pointing to a coffee table surrounded by windows and fat leather armchairs. The table was full of different newspapers, all folded and neatly set out.

Their mum led the way. Iris tried to follow with a particularly grown-up walk, not making any sound with her feet. Kick, of course, clumped over noisily as though he spent his whole life wandering around hotels.

Iris sat next to her mum, sinking deeply into the soft, warm leather of the sofa. She never knew just *sitting* could be so nice.

'All right,' said her mum, rustling through the paper to the back pages. 'Here are the movie ads. Let's see ...'

Iris and Kick grinned at each other. They hardly ever went to the movies at home. Usually they waited until the movies came out on DVD, and then they watched them on the weekend. Seeing a movie at the cinema was a real treat.

Their mum looked at her watch. 'If we leave right now, we can walk into town and be at the cinema in twenty minutes. And the next movie sessions start in half an hour. You guys up for it?'

'Absolutely!' Iris said.

But Kick groaned, 'Do we *have* to walk? Can't we get another taxi?'

Iris pulled a face. *How spoilt is he?* Was he really *complaining?*

But their mum didn't seem annoyed. 'The walk will do us good,' she said as she got to her feet. 'Come on. Let's go.'

Iris, Kick and their mum walked along the very busy and colourful city streets. There was so much to see.

Even Kick stopped dragging his feet and was quiet for once as he took in the new sights.

Iris breathed in. The air smelt different here. Fresher or warmer or breezier, or something. Different, anyway.

'There's the cinema,' Kick said, pointing across the road. 'Can we get a choc-top ice-cream and a super-sized drink?'

Iris gave her brother a dirty look. This was supposed to be the greatest trip ever, but if Kick was going to keep acting spoilt, he could wreck it. Wasn't it enough for him to finish the school term early, catch a plane, stay in a hotel *and* go out in the middle of the day to see a movie with their mum?

Of course, having a choc-top and fizzy drink would be great, but Iris thought it was far better manners to wait and see if their mum brought up the idea herself.

Well, Iris decided, *I'm going to show Mum that at least one of us knows how to behave.*

Chapter Seven

Iris loved going to the movies so much, it almost didn't matter which movie she saw. It felt exciting just lining up for tickets in the dimly lit foyer and standing on the red carpet with the smell of popcorn in the air.

She looked longingly at posters for the movie about an all-girl rock band, but Kick was acting like the robot movie was a done deal. Iris frowned at him. She didn't see why Kick should get his own way in everything. It was true, she wanted to behave, but did that *really* mean she had to watch some stupid robot movie?

Her mum whispered in her ear. 'We'll let him have his way on this one, OK, sweetie? And I'll make it up to you later.'

Iris looked up quickly and said, 'It's OK. I don't mind.'

But that was only *half* true. When Iris thought about her mum, of course she didn't care what movie they saw. When she looked at Kick, though, she felt herself getting angry. He wasn't even nice about getting his own way. Instead, he was jumping around gleefully.

Sometimes she wished she was an only child. It would be much nicer to have her mum all to herself instead of having to be the big sister *all the time*, letting Kick have his own way *again*.

'Iris?' said her mum. 'Are you sure you're OK with Kick's movie?'

Iris realised her face had scrunched up into a scowl again. She took a deep breath and then let it out in a sigh. She looked at her mum.

'Yes,' she said. 'It's fine. Really.'

Maybe she could try to pretend Kick wasn't there. But that wouldn't be easy.

'Hey, Mum,' Kick yelled, even though

he was standing right beside them. 'Can I have some money? I want to line up for choc-tops. And can we have popcorn too? And that drink?'

If I were the deaf one, she thought, *I'd take my hearing aids out now, and switch off Kick's voice like a bad song on the radio.*

After the movie, Iris was starving. The choc-top hadn't filled her up for long. Of course Kick was hungry, too, and he was being really loud about it.

'I want a hamburger,' he said. 'I'm so starving, all I can think about is a hamburger. And chips. And a milkshake. Can we get one, mum? Please?'

Iris's mum bent down and put her hand on Kick's shoulder. 'Slow down, Kick. How about Iris gets a turn to choose?'

'OK,' Kick shrugged. 'Hey, Iris, choose hamburgers, OK? And hot chips with sauce. That's the best choice, OK?'

Iris liked hamburgers as much as Kick did, but right then she felt like doing the exact opposite of whatever he wanted just to spite him. What was the opposite of a hamburger?

'Well, Iris?' said her mum. 'What will it be?'

Iris smiled sweetly. She had an idea that would annoy Kick *and* please her mum.

Perfect! 'I'd *really* love some sushi, actually,' she said.

'Great!' said her mum. 'Exactly what we need after all that junk food.'

Kick groaned, and Iris smiled again.

Suffer, brother! she thought.

Chapter Eight

Walking through the city, Iris felt so hungry that she started to worry that cold rice and seaweed wouldn't be enough to stop her stomach growling. Especially when they kept walking past the delicious smells of hot pizza and kebabs.

But then her mum found a sushi train restaurant.

'It's so cute!' Iris said. She hadn't seen

anything like it before. A miniature train was trundling along around the benches, pulling little carriages of sushi behind it!

'Right, here's what we'll do,' said her mum as they sat down. 'One plate at a time off the train, and finish what you've got before you take another one.'

The little train rattled past them, and Iris's mum took a plate of glistening cubes of raw fish.

'What a good suggestion, Iris,' she said. 'This is lovely.'

Kick piped up, 'I don't want any of this fancy, spicy stuff. Where are the normal tuna rolls like we get at our sushi place at home?'

Iris's mum gave Kick some chicken and avocado sushi, but he kept complaining.

'I'll eat it,' he grumbled. 'But I won't like it. And I still want a hamburger more than ever.'

'Tough, Kick,' Iris snapped. 'It was my choice, and Mum agreed, so there.'

'That's enough,' her mum said firmly. 'Just eat. If you can both behave yourselves for two minutes, I'll order some fat noodles for us all. Will that do?'

'Hey, yeah, cool!' said Kick cheerfully.

Iris, though, was amazed. *Both* behave yourselves? *Both*? How unfair was that? It was Kick that was acting all spoilt, not Iris.

It's Kick's fault, she thought, hurt. *There wouldn't even have been an argument without him.*

I just can't win.

After their fat noodles, their mum took Iris and Kick to the science museum. Normally, Iris would have thought it was fantastic to try out all those machines and gadgets, and Kick seemed to be having a good time, but she was fed up.

It was like there was only room on holiday for one kid. At home, Iris and Kick had worked out how to share things so that it was mostly fair between them. That wasn't happening here, though. Kick was getting everything his own way, and Iris was left with nothing.

Well, I guess we all know which kid this holiday is really for, she thought sulkily.

Chapter Nine

The next morning, Iris was dressed and choosing a ribbon for her new hairstyle when room service knocked on the door with breakfast.

The hotel waiter pushed a trolley full of food into their room and checked off their order. Iris was having scrambled eggs and sausages.

Iris's dad had gone to pick up a hire car

to drive everyone to Nan and Pa's, while the rest of them had packed their bags, ready to check out of the hotel.

Iris got a secret, naughty thrill at the thought of leaving all the beds unmade and the towels on the bed, and she had one tiny wrapped soap tucked safely in her bag.

Iris ran up the path to her nan and pa's house and banged on the door.

'Nan and Pa!' she yelled through the glass panels.

Kick thumped down the path behind her. 'Nan!' he bellowed, standing next to Iris on the top step. 'Mum got you flowers!'

Iris elbowed him. 'Don't say that! It was meant to be a surprise!'

'It doesn't matter, Iris,' her mum said, shaking her head. 'The flowers will be just as pretty whether they're a surprise or not.'

Then the front door opened and Iris saw her nan and pa. She loved it how they always came to the door together, as though they were so excited to see Iris and Kick that neither of them could wait in the kitchen.

'Here you are, my little darlings!' cried her nan, coming out onto the porch to hug them before they could even get into the house.

'Let me look at them,' said her pa, coming through the door. Iris and Kick both wriggled out of their nan's hug to cuddle with their pa instead.

'Good grief!' he said, making an amazed face at Iris's mum. 'Who *are* these people? I thought you were bringing little Iris and Kick, and instead you've come with some beautiful young lady and this huge bruiser of a man.'

Iris laughed and rolled her eyes. 'Oh, Pa!'

'Oh, it *is* you, Rissy!' he chuckled.

Iris's dad struggled down the path with some of the bags from the car.

Her pa called out to him, 'Christopher, my boy! I think you've grown, too! Come over here, son, and let me see those muscles.'

Iris giggled. It was so weird to hear her pa teasing her dad like he was still a little boy.

Especially because that was exactly how her dad teased her and Kick!

'Come on,' said her nan. 'The bags can wait, but my caramel slice can't.'

'Caramel slice!' yelled Kick, bounding inside.

'Yes, and coconut biscuits and sultana cake, too,' her nan said, smiling at Iris. 'Just something for you to nibble on while we get lunch ready.'

Iris grinned. She followed her nan down the long corridor to the kitchen, past framed photos of her and Kick as babies, and of their cousins, Lauren and Nigella, who lived in England and went to boarding school.

They reached the kitchen and their pa said, 'You'd better sit down, kids. Nan won't be happy until she sees you eating. The coconut biscuits are for you, Rissy.'

Iris glanced at her mum. At home, they weren't allowed sweet things until way after lunch.

But her mum smiled and shrugged. 'It's a holiday,' she said. 'And your nan's gone to a lot of trouble.'

Iris grinned. She didn't need to be told twice!

Chapter Ten

'So what are you going to do while you're here?' Iris's pa asked them.

'*I'd* like to see the new display at the art gallery,' her mum said, jumping in straight away. 'And then I thought we could take the kids over to the war memorial.'

Kick snorted. 'Bo-*ring*! Can I stay here with Pa and watch telly instead?'

Iris glared at him.

'Kick!' said her mum, sounding impatient with him at last. 'We haven't decided what we're doing yet, but whatever it is, you're coming with us. We'll have a good time.'

'Oh, please? Pretty please? I'll be good,' he said, looking pleadingly at their dad instead.

Iris watched them all exchanging looks over Kick's head. Iris knew that Kick was about to get his own way again.

'Well ...' said her mum.

'Ah, he'll be terrific,' said her pa. 'We'll watch the game on TV and he can help with dinner.'

'Yesss!' Kick cheered.

'Why don't you kids get the rest of the

bags out of the car while Mum and I talk to Nan and Pa for a minute?' their dad said, throwing Iris the keys. 'You know where your bedroom is.'

Iris snatched the keys out of the air and strode down the corridor, not caring if Kick was keeping up with her or not. She carefully and quietly opened the front door, but then stomped grumpily down the path to the car.

Kick came and stood beside her as she opened the boot and started hauling the bags out.

'Don't give me Dad's bag,' he said. 'It's way too heavy. I'll take Mum's and mine.'

'Anything else?' Iris said crossly.

'What's *your* problem?' Kick said.

'You!' she hissed. 'You're selfish, and bratty, and acting like the whole holiday is about you getting everything you want – *that's* what!'

Kick shrugged. 'Whatever, *Rissy*.'

'Don't!' she growled. 'That's Pa's name for me. No-one else's.'

'OK, Rissy,' he laughed. 'Sorry, Rissy. I won't do it again, Rissy. I didn't realise you were the boss of me, Rissy.'

'I'm warning you, Drop-Kick,' she said, pointing her finger at him.

'Oooh, like I'm *so* scared, Rissy!'

With a little scream of frustration, Iris jumped over the bags at her feet and punched her brother in the shoulder. 'You brat!'

Kick fell backwards over the edge of the gutter and sat down hard on the nature strip. 'Ow!' he yelled, clutching his leg. 'Look what you've done!'

This will stop you complaining!

'You're not hurt,' said Iris, narrowing her eyes. 'You're just noisy and sooky and a pain in the bum!'

'What's going on here?' said a cross voice behind her. Iris looked up to see her mum, dad, nan and pa all standing by the garden gate, staring at her with surprise and disappointment.

'Iris! What have you done?' their mum said as she knelt down beside Kick.

Chapter Eleven

Iris threw herself down on the bed in her nan and pa's spare room. She was sharing the room with Kick, but he was smart enough to stay out of her way for now.

She couldn't remember ever being so angry. It was just so completely unfair. Kick had been a pain the whole trip, but now *she* was the one getting in trouble.

All they care about is their precious Kick,

Iris thought bitterly. *Like he's a helpless little baby, when he's actually just a giant brat!*

Iris could hear Kick out in the kitchen, acting extra charming and funny and saying *please* and *thank you very much* about a million times a minute.

As if Nan and Pa haven't already figured out who the good kid is, she thought grumpily. She rolled over towards the wall. *I might as well not even be here.*

Then she felt her bed sag as someone walked in and sat on the end of it. She ignored whoever it was.

'Iris?' It was her mum.

Iris lay still and pretended not to hear.

'Iris, come on. I want to talk to you.'

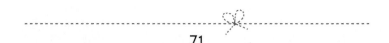

Iris rolled over very slowly and sat up without looking properly at her mum.

'Kick's laying it on a bit thick out there,' her mum whispered. 'I think he's trying to make up for his appalling manners earlier.'

I thought I'd be in big trouble.

Iris frowned. 'Huh?'

'Oh, yes,' her mum said, 'you're not the only one who's noticed how ordinary his behaviour's been so far. And you're not the only one who's embarrassed, either.'

Now Iris was really surprised. 'Who else is embarrassed?'

'Kick is!' her mum said. 'After you ran inside, Pa told him to pick himself up and stop making such a racket. And Nan asked him what on earth he'd done to make you so cross. And then Dad made him bring in all the bags by himself.'

Iris was amazed. 'You were all on my side? But I was sure everyone was totally disappointed in me.'

'Well, I wouldn't say we were exactly *proud* of you for whacking your little brother, but we do understand. He's been one demanding boy.'

Iris gulped and said, 'So I haven't wrecked the holiday? Not completely?'

Her mum laughed and hugged her. 'Honey, it's a *family* holiday, and you can't wreck family as easily as that! No, we're going to have a great holiday. I just need you to take it a little easier and enjoy yourself. It's not up to you to make sure Kick is behaving. Leave that to Dad and me, OK?'

'OK,' Iris smiled.

Iris heard her nan calling out, 'Is everyone ready for lunch?'

Iris jumped up off the bed. 'Coming, Nan!'

Chapter Twelve

To Iris's surprise, before she could say sorry to Kick for hitting him, he came up to her while she was washing her hands for lunch.

'Sorry, Iris,' he mumbled. 'I've been a pain.'

'Wow,' she said, staring at him. 'Thanks. I'm sorry, too. And thanks for saying sorry first. That's cool of you.'

He grinned at her. 'Yeah, I am cool. Plus, Nan said if I didn't make up with you she wouldn't let me have any pudding tonight.'

'There's pudding?' Iris grinned back. 'Which one?'

'The chocolate one that makes its own sauce in the dish.'

Iris nodded. 'Oh, yeah, that one's worth saying the first sorry.'

Iris couldn't help giggling to herself at the lunch table. It was so obvious that Kick was trying to be on his best behaviour. He was being way too polite.

We can still have an awesome holiday!

'So, what are we doing this afternoon?' her dad asked.

Iris and Kick looked at each other.

I really don't want to go to the war memorial or the art gallery like Mum suggested, but I'm not going to be the one to say so, Iris thought. She knew Kick was thinking exactly the same thing.

Their dad looked at them both, waiting for someone to say something. Iris bit her lip.

Her dad laughed and turned to her mum. 'Well, that's a huge vote of interest from the kids for the idea you came up with, darling!' he told her.

'I think it'll be extremely interesting,' their mum protested.

Without meaning to, Iris snorted in disbelief.

'Iris!' her mum gasped. 'You know, things *can* be more fun than they sound at first.

I reckon you kids would be surprised.'

'Amazed, even,' said Kick, rolling his eyes.

Iris choked back a giggle. She'd been so focused on Kick being bratty, she'd forgotten how funny he could be.

'All right then,' her mum said, throwing her hands up. 'I'm keeping out of it. You three decide what we're going to do.'

Iris's dad grinned. 'What do you think, kids? Fairy floss at the fun park? Roller-blading in the city gardens? Or how about we find one of those horse-drawn carriages and ride around town?'

Iris wanted to hug him. It was like the holiday had begun all over again, and everyone was getting a second chance. Her mum had been right – the holiday wasn't wrecked.

I guess that's what she means about a family holiday, Iris thought.

A family holiday didn't have to be completely perfect, and not everyone had to be completely happy every second of the day. But they were all together, whatever they were doing. Whether that was going roller-blading or having a fight.

Chapter Thirteen

Iris had to admit that Kick was still slightly painful some of the time, but then again, he *was* her little brother. It wasn't his fault he was less mature than her.

Plus, the holiday wouldn't have been nearly as much fun without him. In fact, his pushiness was even useful. There was no way Iris would have begged for a show bag after spending the whole day at the fun park, but Kick did. And their dad agreed to buy them one each!

And Kick could be sweet, too. Like asking their mum for two dollars at the fudge factory, so he could sneak off and buy Iris a lollipop shaped like a saxophone.

It was even fun sharing a room with him. She thought it might have been spooky if she had to sleep alone. Her nan's old porcelain doll was pretty in the daytime, but Iris didn't like how creepy its glass eyes looked in the dark. And there were some weird creaking sounds in the roof, too. But none of that bothered her with Kick in the room.

There was just one problem. The

holiday was slipping by too fast now that everything was going so well. The afternoon Iris spent trudging around the science museum in a bad mood had felt like it lasted for six months. But the next six *days* of their holiday were so full of excitement, they went by in a flash.

'We need more time,' she complained to Kick. 'I'm not ready to go back yet. It feels like we just got to Nan and Pa's.'

'And I want heaps more time hanging out with Dad without him going off to work,' Kick said.

'Exactly,' Iris agreed.

On the last day, Iris and Kick sadly zipped up their bags. Iris checked under the beds for anything they'd forgotten.

'Time to go, kids,' their dad called. 'Say goodbye to Nan and Pa.'

That's the worst bit, Iris realised. *Now that the family holiday's over, we have to leave some of our family behind.*

Iris dragged her bag out of the bedroom, and saw her nan wiping her eyes as she handed Iris's mum three plastic containers and said, 'Just some fruit cake, scones and biscuits for when you get home.'

That made Iris smile, even though she felt sad.

'Cheer up, Rissy,' said her pa, giving her a bear hug. 'Nan and I were talking with your dad, and we're planning on coming to visit you lot for a holiday very soon.'

'Really? How soon?' Iris asked excitedly.

Her pa kissed her on the nose. '*Soon soon.*'

'Come on, Iris,' Kick said, bumping into her. 'Remember, I've got the window seat for take-off this time.'

Iris grinned. *That's right, the plane ride home! The holiday's over, but there's still more to look forward to!*

'Did you have a good time?' her nan asked as they hugged by the car.

After a shaky start to their trip, Iris was glad she could answer truthfully.

'The best!' she said. 'This was the ultimate holiday!'

Sleep-over

Boy friend?

Surf's Up

Sister Spirit

Dancing Queen

Flower Girl

Camp Chaos

Best Christmas Ever

Back to School

The Worst Gymnast

Sink or Swim

Music Mad

Class Captain

The New Girl

Karate Kicks

Secret's Out